U0022392

Tashi and the Ghosts
© Text, Anna Fienberg and Barbara Fienberg 1996
© Illustrations, Kim Gamble 1996
First published in 1996 by Allen & Unwin Pty Ltd., Australia

•大喜說故事系列•

THE MOUNTAIN OF WHITE TIGERS

前進白虎嶺

Anna Fienberg
Barbara Fienberg　著

Kim Gamble　繪

王秋瑩　譯

三民書局

The doorbell rang.

'I'll go,' Jack called, because he knew who it would be. Tashi was spending the day with him, and they were going for a **ferry** ride. Jack had said to come early, in time for breakfast.

門鈴響了。

「我去開門，」傑克喊著，因為他知道是誰來了。大喜會整天和他在一起，他們要搭渡船去玩。傑克叫他早點兒來，好趕上吃早餐的時間。

ferry [ˋfɛrɪ] 名 渡船

But when Tashi walked in, Mom **peered at** his face with a worried **frown**. 'You look a bit **pale** this morning, Tashi,' she said.

'Yes, I know,' sighed Tashi. 'I've been up **burping** Ghost Pie all night.'

'**Pancakes** coming!' cried Dad from the kitchen. Tashi turned a little paler.

不過在大喜進來的時候，老媽仔細地看了看他愁眉苦臉的樣子。「你今天早上看起來臉色不太好，大喜，」她說。

　　「嗯，我知道，」大喜嘆了口氣。「我吃了鬼派後整晚沒睡，一直打嗝。」

　　「煎餅來囉！」老爸的聲音從廚房傳來。

　　大喜的臉變得更蒼白了。

peer at　凝視
frown [fraʊn]　名 愁眉苦臉
pale [pel]　形 蒼白的
burp [bɝp]　動 打嗝
pancake [`pæn,kek]　名 煎餅

When they were all sitting around the table in the garden, and Tashi had **managed** three pancakes after all, Jack decided that he'd waited long enough. 'How did you meet this **Wicked Baron**?'

當他們在花園裡圍著桌子坐著時，大喜最後還是吃了三塊煎餅，傑克覺得等的夠久了。「你是怎麼遇見這壞地主的啊？」

manage [`mænɪdʒ] 勔 吃光

wicked [`wɪkəd] 形 壞的

baron [`bærən] 名 大地主

'Well, it was like this,' said Tashi. 'One day I went to visit Li Tam, my favorite **auntie**. I always like going to her place because she has the most interesting house in the village. The rooms are all **decorated** with painted **scrolls** and she lets me touch the **delicate** bowls and vases and hand-carved swords.'

「這個嘛，事情是這樣的，」大喜說。「有一天我去看我最喜歡的李甜阿姨。我很喜歡去她家，因為她家是村裡最有趣的房子。房間全裝飾著畫卷，而且她還讓我摸摸精緻的碗、花瓶和手工雕刻的劍。」

auntie [`æntɪ] 名 阿姨（aunt的親切稱呼）
decorate [`dɛkəˌret] 動 裝飾 《with》
scroll [skrol] 名 卷軸
delicate [`dɛləkət] 形 精緻的

'Does Li Tam do a lot of sword-**fighting**?'
asked Dad.

Jack rolled his eyes, but Tashi just smiled. 'No,
the swords **belonged to** her father. Anyway,'
he went on, 'this particular day I didn't even
get a **chance** to knock on the door, when it was
flung open and out stormed Li Tam's
landlord, the wicked Baron.'

'Aha!' cried Mom and Dad.

'Yes, he was **grinding** his gold teeth, and he pushed me out of the way. I picked myself up and as I **dusted** my pants off, I **wondered** why the Baron looked so angry.'

「李甜常比劍嗎？」老爸問。

傑克翻了翻眼珠子，大喜只是笑了笑。「沒有，劍是她爸爸的。總之，」大喜繼續說，「就在那一天，我還沒來得及敲門，門忽然被甩開了，李甜的地主——那壞地主衝了出來。」

「啊哈！」老爸老媽同時叫了出來。

fight [faɪt] 勔 戰鬥
belong to 屬於
chance [tʃæns] 名 機會
fling [flɪŋ] 勔 粗暴地摔擲
landlord [ˋlændˏlɔrd] 名 地主

「沒錯，那時他咬牙切齒，一把把我推開。我從地上站了起來，一邊拍拍褲子上的灰塵，一邊納悶大地主為什麼看起來這麼生氣。」

grind [graɪnd] 勔 摩擦
dust [dʌst] 勔 抹去灰塵 《off》
wonder [`wʌndɚ] 勔 對…感到疑惑

'Was he a friend of Li Tam's?' asked Dad.

'Oh no!' said Tashi. 'He was no one's friend. The only thing he loved was gold. You see, this Baron had once been poor, but he had **tricked** an old banker out of his riches, and then he had stolen some money here and hired a few pirates there, until he had a huge **fortune**.'

'Where did he keep all his gold?' asked Mom.

'Well, it was a great **mystery**,' said Tashi. 'The people in the village were certain that he had **hidden** it away in a deep cave. But no one could be quite sure because the cave lay at the top of The Mountain of White Tigers.'

'I've never seen a white tiger,' said Dad, 'but I've heard they are the **fiercest** kind.'

「他是李甜的朋友嗎？」老爸問。

「哦，不是的！」大喜說。「他沒有任何朋友。他只愛金子。你們知道嗎，這個大地主本來很窮，不過他騙走了一位老銀行家的財產，接著這裡偷了一些錢，那裡僱了一些海盜，最後他就有了一大筆的財富。」

「他把金子全放在哪兒呢？」老媽問。

「唔，這是個大祕密，」大喜說。

「村子裡的人確定他把金子藏在一個深深的洞裡面。不過沒有人能很確定，因為那個洞是在白虎嶺上。」

「我從沒見過白老虎，」老爸說，「不過我聽說牠們是最兇猛的一種老虎。」

trick [trɪk] 勔 騙（人）
fortune [`fɔrtʃən] 名 財富
mystery [`mɪstrɪ] 名 神秘
hide [haɪd] 勔 隱藏（過去分詞 hidden [`hɪdn̩]）
fierce [fɪrs] 形 兇猛的

'Yes,' said Tashi. 'Anyway, Li Tam was very
upset after the Baron stormed out. She told me
that he had called to tell her that she would
have to leave her home at once because he had
been **offered** a good price **for** it. And Li Tam
had cried out, "Why must you have *my* house?
You own the whole village!" But the Baron
had ordered her to pack her bags by the end of
the week.

「沒錯，」大喜說。「總而言之，在大地主衝了出去以後，李甜很懊惱。她告訴我大地主來叫她馬上搬家，因為有人出高價要買。李甜哭了起來，『為什麼你非得要我的房子呢？你擁有全村哪！』不過大地主已經命令她在這禮拜之前收拾好行李。

upset [ʌpˈsɛt] 形 心煩的
offer...for 開價

'"Look at this then!" Li Tam had told him, and she'd pulled a piece of paper from the hidden **drawer** in her **cupboard**. On it was written a **promise** from the old banker that she could stay in the house for as long as she **pleased**.

'The Baron's face had grown red and that is why he'd stormed out, knocking me over as he went. But Li Tam was worried. "Tashi," she said to me, "I just know he won't stop at this. He'll try to find a way to push me out of my home."

「『那麼看看這個吧！』李甜對大地主說，她從櫥櫃的隱密抽屜裡拿出了一份文件來，上頭寫的是那老銀行家答應李甜這房子她愛住多久就可以住多久。

　　「大地主漲紅了臉，這就是為什麼他衝出去，還把我撞倒的原因。但是李甜很擔心。『大喜，』她對我說，『我知道他不會就此罷休的。他會想法子把我趕出這個房子的。』

drawer [drɔr] 名 抽屜

cupboard [`kʌbəd] 名 櫥櫃

promise [`prɑmɪs] 名 承諾

please [pliz] 動 喜歡

'And sure enough, the next day when I
went to visit her, I found the house was
alive with mice. And they were everywhere.
All the tables and chairs, shelves and
cupboards seemed to be moving, crawling
with **wriggling** bodies. From under beds,
inside wardrobes, came loud **squeals** and
scratchings. Well, Li Tam ran to me and
said, "Look what the Baron has done! He
sent his **servants** during the night to **tip**
sacks of mice in through the windows."

'"Don't worry, Auntie," I said, "I will fix it." I ran home for a bag of rice cakes. I **crumbled** them up and laid a trail of **crumbs** from Li Tam's house right up to the Baron's kitchen door. The mice **scrambled** after me, **gobbling** up the crumbs as they went. And soon it was the *Baron* who had a houseful of mice.

「果然，隔天我去看她的時候，發現整間房子都是
老鼠。到處都是。所有的桌子、椅子、架子和櫥櫃似乎
都在動，爬滿了蠕動的小身體。從床底下、從衣櫃裡傳
來吵鬧的吱吱聲和東抓西抓的聲音。李甜跑來跟我說，
『看大地主幹的好事！他派僕人趁晚上把好幾袋的老鼠
從窗戶倒進來。』

alive with　充滿
wriggle [`rɪgl̩] 動 蠕動
squeal [skwil] 名 尖銳叫聲
servant [`sɝvənt] 名 僕人
tip [tɪp] 動 倒（東西）

「『別擔心，阿姨，』我說，『我來搞定。』我跑回家拿了一袋米糕。我把它們弄碎，然後從李甜家往大地主家的廚房門口一路灑下去。那些老鼠在我後面搶來搶去，邊走邊把沿路的碎屑吃了。不一會兒便換成大地主有一屋子的老鼠了。

crumble [`krʌmbl̩] 動 弄成碎屑
crumb [krʌm] 名 碎屑
scramble [`skræmbl̩] 動 爭先恐後地搶
gobble [`gɑbl̩] 動 大口大口地吃 《up》

'He was **furious**—roaring like a bull with a **bellyache**!—and when he saw the villagers laughing at him behind their hands, he **charged** right into the square on market day and shouted to them, "Tomorrow is the day you pay your rent money. **From now on**, all your rent will be three times as much as before. Be sure to have the money ready!" The people were shocked. "What will we do?" they **wailed**. "We have nothing more to give!"

「他氣死了——像肚子痛的野牛一樣大吼大叫！——當他看見村民偷偷地嘲笑他，就氣得衝到市集廣場上對著村民大叫，『明天是你們付租金的日子。從現在起，你們要付三倍的租金。給我把錢準備好！』村民嚇壞了。『我們要怎麼辦？』他們放聲哭泣著說。『我們沒有那麼多錢來付租金啊！』

furious [`fjʊrɪəs] 形 很生氣的

bellyache [`bɛlɪˌek] 名 肚子痛

charge [tʃɑrdʒ] 動 猛衝

from now on 從今以後

wail [wel] 動 放聲哭泣

31

'When I ran to tell Li Tam she said, "Oh, Tashi, if only we had the money to buy our own houses, then we would never have to worry about the wicked Baron again."'

'Aha!' cried Mom and Dad and Jack together.

'Aha!' agreed Tashi. 'That's when I felt one of my **clever** ideas coming on. So that night, when the last light went out, I **crept** through the streets to the Baron's house and **tapped** on the kitchen window. Third Aunt, who was the Baron's cook, opened the door.

「我跑去告訴李甜，她說，『噢，大喜，如果我們有錢買下自己的房子，那我們就再也不用害怕那個壞地主了。』」

「啊哈！」爸媽和傑克一起叫了起來。

「啊哈！」大喜附和著。「就在那時我想到了一個好點子。於是那天晚上，趁著天黑，我悄悄地穿過街道，來到大地主家，輕輕地敲廚房的窗戶。我那在大地主家當廚子的三嬸開了門。

clever [ˋklɛvɚ] 形 聰明的

creep [krip] 動 躡手躡腳地走路

tap [tæp] 動 輕敲 《on》

'"Auntie, please let me in," I **whispered**. I ran over to the table where I'd often sat on baking mornings and pulled away the **rug** that lay under it. There was a little door over a **flight** of steps leading down into darkness.

「『嬸嬸，拜託讓我進去，』我低聲說著。我衝到我在有烤麵包的早晨常常來坐的桌子，拉開下面的地毯。有一道小門蓋在一段通往黑暗的階梯上。

whisper [`hwɪspɚ] 勔 低語

rug [rʌg] 名 地毯

flight [flaɪt] 名 階梯

'"You can't go down there, Tashi," said Third Aunt. "That **passage** leads all the way to the Mountain of White Tigers, and no one has ever returned from there."

'"The Baron must have," I said, "so I expect I will **manage** it, too." Still, as I peered into the blackness below, I did feel just a little afraid.'

'I don't wonder,' **shivered** Dad. 'Sometimes I feel a little afraid just going to put the **garbage** out at night.'

「『你不能下去，大喜，』」三嬸說。「『這地道一直通到白虎嶺，沒有人從那裡回來過。』」

「『大地主一定有過，』我說，『所以我想我也可以。』」可是，我看了看下面黑漆漆的一片，還是覺得有點兒害怕。」

「那不奇怪，」老爸發著抖說。「有時我只是晚上出去倒垃圾，都會有點怕怕的。」

passage [`pæsɪdʒ] 名 通道
manage [`mænɪdʒ] 動 設法完成
shiver [`ʃɪvɚ] 動 發抖
garbage [`gɑrbɪdʒ] 名 垃圾

'Well,' said Tashi, 'I stopped looking into the dark and I whispered, "Hand me your **lamp**, please, Auntie. I'll be back before the Baron comes down to his breakfast in the morning."'

'The passage **twisted** and turned, **winding** like a rabbit's **burrow** deep into the earth. I held my lamp high, but I could only see a short way in front of me, and the blackness ahead looked like the end of the world.

'I must **admit** that once or twice I did think of going back. I had no idea how long I'd been walking, or how much time I had left.

「嗯，」大喜說，「我不再往下看那黑黑的一片，我低聲說：『嬸嬸，拜託把油燈給我。我會在明天早上大地主下來吃早餐以前回來。』

　　「那通道彎彎曲曲的，就像地底下的兔子窩繞來繞去的。我把油燈舉得高高的，可是還是只能看見我前面的一小段路，前面黑黑的看起來就像世界的盡頭。

　　「我得承認我曾經有一、兩次想要回頭。我不知道我走了多遠，或是走了多久。

lamp [læmp] 名 油燈

twist [twɪst] 動 彎曲

wind [waɪnd] 動 彎曲

burrow [`bɝo] 名 巢穴

admit [əd`mɪt] 動 承認

'But at last I felt the ground **slope** upwards, and
I could feel my heart start **thumping** hard as I
climbed up the steep path—and suddenly, at the
top, I stopped. The path was **blocked**. I held up
my lamp and saw a door, with a gold **latch**. I
pulled at it and *whoosh!*—the door **swung** open.

「不過最後我感覺地面往上傾，我一邊爬陡峭的小路，一邊可以感覺我的心臟開始撲通撲通用力地跳著——突然，在最上面的地方，我停了下來。路被堵住了。我舉起油燈，看見一個有黃金門閂的門，我拉了一下門閂，呼的一聲——門突然打開了。

slope [slop] 動 傾斜

thump [θʌmp] 動 （心臟）撲通撲通跳

block [blɑk] 動 堵住

latch [lætʃ] 名 門鎖

swing [swɪŋ] 動 （門）轉動成⋯狀態

'I stepped out onto the Mountain of White Tigers.

'My face **tingled** in the snowy air and I looked **nervously** into the night. The lamp showed me a path, but on each side of it were tall black trees, and behind those trees who knew *what* was waiting!

'But I couldn't bear to go back empty-handed. And just then, I heard a **growl**, deep as thunder. I peered into the dark, but I could see nothing, only hear a grinding of teeth, like stones scraping. The growling became roaring, and my ears were ringing with the noise, and then, right in front of me, a white **shape** came out from behind a tree, and then another and another. The tigers were coming!

「我走出去踏上了白虎嶺。

「冰冷的空氣刺痛了我的臉，我緊張兮兮地看了看眼前黑漆漆的一片。油燈照亮了一條小路，不過小路兩邊都是高高的黑森林，誰知道在這些樹後面有什麼東西等著我！

tingle [`tɪŋgl̩] 動 感到刺痛

nervously [`nɝvəslɪ] 副 焦躁不安地

「可是我不能空手而回。就在這時候，我聽到一聲低吼，像打雷一樣沈悶。我往黑黑的地方看了看，不過什麼都沒看見，只聽見像磨石頭那樣的磨牙聲。那低吼聲變成了咆哮聲，教我的耳朵嗡嗡作響，接著，就在我面前，有個白影子從樹後面出來，一個接著一個。是老虎來了！

bear [bɛr] 動 忍受
growl [graʊl] 名 吼叫聲
scrape [skrep] 動 刮出刺耳聲
ring [rɪŋ] 動 （耳朵）嗡嗡作響
shape [ʃep] 名 形狀，樣子

'They came so close to me that I could see their **whiskers**, silver in the moonlight, and their great red eyes, glowing like fires. They were even fiercer than I had been told, and their teeth were even sharper in their dark wet mouths, but I was ready for them. Second Aunt had warned me that the one thing white tigers fear is fire. 'I took a big breath and swung my bright burning lamp round and around my head. I charged down the path roaring, "Aargh! Aargh!" till my **lungs** were **bursting**.

「牠們靠得我好近，在月光下，我可以看見牠們銀色的鬍鬚，和牠們紅色的大眼睛像火焰般熊熊燃燒。牠們甚至比我聽說的還要兇猛，而且那又黑又溼的嘴巴裡的牙齒也比我聽說的更尖，不過我已經準備好對付牠們了。二嬸曾提醒我說，白老虎怕火。

「我深呼吸了一下，然後在我的頭頂揮舞那盞燃燒發亮的油燈。我衝下小路大叫著，『啊喝！啊喝！』喊到我的肺都快要爆掉了。

whisker [`hwɪskɚ] 名 鬍鬚
glowing [`gloɪŋ] 形 燃燒般發亮的
sharp [ʃɑrp] 形 尖銳的
lung [lʌŋ] 名 肺
burst [bɝst] 動 爆裂

'The tigers stopped and **stared at** me. They must have thought I was a whirling demon, with circles of light streaking about their heads. They bared their teeth, growling like drums rolling. But I saw them **flinch**, their white coats shivering over their muscles, and slowly, one by one, they turned away, gliding back through the trees. Oh, I was so happy watching those white shapes **disappearing**! I ran on and there, **looming up** above me, was the mouth of the cave.

'The **entrance** was blocked by a huge stone boulder. I tried to squeeze through but the gap was too small.'

「那些老虎停了下來，盯著我看。牠們一定認為我是一個旋轉惡魔，頭上有光環飛旋。牠們露出了牙齒，像打鼓一般地咆哮著。可是我看到牠們退縮了，牠們白色的毛皮隨著身體肌肉顫抖著，一個接一個慢慢地轉身走了，悄悄地穿過樹林溜走了。哦，看著那些白色東西消失，我好高興哦！我繼續跑，就在那上頭隱約出現了一個洞口。

　　「入口被一個大圓石堵住了。我試著擠進去，可是那縫隙太小了。」

stare at 盯著看

flinch [flɪntʃ] 動 退縮

disappear [ˌdɪsə`pɪr] 動 消失

loom up 隱約出現

entrance [`ɛntrəns] 名 入口

'Did you have to turn back then, Tashi?' Jack held his breath.

'I thought for a moment I'd have to,' Tashi **nodded**. 'But then I remembered that I'd popped a piece of Ghost Pie into my pocket before leaving home. I quickly **nibbled** a bit and pushed at the boulder again. This time my hand slid right through it and the rest of me followed as easily as stepping through shadows.

「那你只好回頭了嗎，大喜？」傑克摒住呼吸。

「我一時以為我只能回頭，」大喜點點頭。「不過後來我想起我出門前放了一片鬼派在口袋裡。我很快地咬了一小口，再推一次那大圓石。這次我的手穿過了圓石，身體的其他部分就像穿過影子一般，很容易就穿了過去。

nod [nɑd] 勔 點頭

pop [pɑp] 勔 猛然放下

nibble [`nɪbl̩] 勔 一點一點地吃

'I ran inside *whooping*! There were sacks and sacks of shiny, golden coins! **Puffing and panting**, I loaded them into a huge **knapsack** I had with me, and **hauled** it onto my back to carry.'

「我跑了進去，耶！──有一袋又一袋閃閃發亮的金幣耶！我上氣不接下氣地把金幣放進我隨身攜帶的大背包裡，把它拉到背上帶走。」

whoop [hup] 勔 歡呼

puff and pant 氣喘吁吁

load [lod] 勔 裝入 《into》

knapsack [`næp,sæk] 名 輕便背包

haul [hɔl] 勔 拖拉

'I wish *I'd* been there to help you!' Jack said
wistfully.

'Me too,' said Tashi. 'That knapsack made my
knees buckle. And then, coming out of the
cave, I had to whirl my lamp round my head
and roar as well, **just in case** there were still
tigers **lurking** in the trees.'

'So how did you crawl back through the **tunnel**
with all that gold on your back?' asked Mum.

「真希望我在那裡幫你！」傑克渴望地說。

「我也希望，」大喜說。「那背包重得讓我的膝蓋站都站不直。然後，我出了山洞，我也得在頭上揮舞油燈，鬼吼鬼叫，以防老虎還躲在樹林裡。

「那你是怎麼背著全部的金幣，穿過地道爬回去的呢？」老媽問。

wistfully [`wɪstfəlɪ] 副 渴望地

buckle [`bʌkl̩] 動 彎曲

just in case 以防萬一

lurk [lɝk] 動 埋伏

tunnel [`tʌnl̩] 名 地道

'Well, it was like this,' said Tashi. 'I took the sack off my back and put it on the ground. Then I rolled it along with my feet. It was easier that way, but very slow. And **of course** I was getting very **worried about** the time.

'I crept back up the stairs and into the kitchen as it was growing light. Third Aunt was just putting a match to the kitchen fire, and she almost dropped the **poker** when she saw me.

'"What a clever Tashi," she cried, when she **spied** the gold.

「這個嘛，事情是這樣的，」大喜說，「我把袋子從背上拿下來，把它放在地上，然後，用腳來滾動袋子。這樣子輕鬆多了，可是卻很慢。當然我越來越擔心時間不夠。

　　「我爬上樓梯，回到廚房，剛好天亮了。三嬸正要升廚火，當她看見我的時候，手中的火鉗差點掉到地上。

　　「當她看見那些金幣的時候，不禁大叫，『多聰明的大喜啊！』」

match [mætʃ] 名 火柴
drop [drɑp] 動 掉落
poker [`pokə] 名 火鉗
spy [spaɪ] 動 看見

'Well, I thanked her, but I wasn't **finished** yet, oh no! I crept to each house in the village and whispered a few words, passing a little sack of gold through the windows.

'Next morning all the people were in the square when the Wicked Baron arrived for his rent. Wise-As-An-Owl stepped **forward**. "Baron," he began, "our children who went away to other parts for work have done well and sent gold home to their families. Now we would like to buy our houses."

「嗯，我向她道謝，不過事情還沒完呢！我悄悄地來到每個村民的家，低聲說了幾句話，就從窗戶遞一小袋金子進去。

　　「隔天早上，當壞地主來收租金的時候，大夥兒全在廣場。聰明道人走向前說：『大地主，我們的孩子在外地事業有成，送了些金子回家。現在我們想要買下自己的房子。』

'And all the villagers stepped up and poured the gold onto the table before the Baron. What a sight it was! The mountain of coins **glittered** so brightly in the morning sun that I had to turn my eyes away! But The Baron stared. He couldn't *stop* looking! Still, he was **hesitating**. He liked getting money every month from his rents, but he couldn't **resist** the sight of all those shining, winking coins. "Very well," he agreed, and I could tell he was itching to gather up the coins and run his fingers through them. "I'll sign right now," and he took the papers that Wise-As-An-Owl had ready for him.

'That night there was a great feast with music and dancing to **celebrate** the new **freedom** of the village. My grandmother and Second Aunt were singing so loudly, that only I heard the faint bellow of rage coming from the Mountain of White Tigers.'

「所有的村民走上前去，把金子倒在大地主前面的桌子上。多壯觀哪！那堆金幣山在早晨的陽光下是如此耀眼閃亮，讓我沒辦法直視！可是大地主看得目不轉睛。他沒法兒不看！但是他有點猶豫不決。他喜歡每個月來收租金，不過他沒辦法抵抗那些閃閃發亮的金幣。『很好，』他同意了，我看得出來他是急著想拿拿這些錢幣，用他的手指摸一摸。

『我現在馬上簽，』他拿起聰明道人為他準備好的文件。

「當晚大家又唱又跳，慶祝村子重獲自由。我奶奶和二嬸唱得好大聲，所以只有我聽到模模糊糊的咆哮聲從白虎嶺傳來。」

glitter [ˋglɪtɚ] 動 閃閃發光
hesitate [ˋhɛzə,tet] 動 猶豫
resist [rɪˋzɪst] 動 抗拒
celebrate [ˋsɛlə,bret] 動 慶祝
freedom [ˋfridəm] 名 自由

'Oh well,' said Dad, 'that wicked Baron got what he **deserved**, eh, Tashi? And I suppose all the village people were happy and **contented** from that day on.'

'Oh yes,' agreed Tashi, 'and so was I, until I came **face to face** with the **Genie**. But now we'd better go—if we don't run all the way we'll miss the ferry! Are you coming, Jack?'

And the two boys raced out the door, as if the Genie itself were after them.

「哦，那，」老爸說，「那壞地主活該，對不對，大喜？我相信村民們從那天起過著幸福滿足的日子了。」

　　「噢，是啊，」大喜附和著，「我也是，一直到我碰上了精靈。不過現在我們最好走了──我們得一路用跑的才趕得上渡船！要走了嗎，傑克？」

　　這兩男孩衝出了門，好似精靈真的在他們後面追著一樣。

deserve [dɪ`zɝv] 動 應得
contented [kən`tɛntɪd] 形 滿足的
face to face 面對面
genie [`dʒinɪ] 名 精靈

小普羅藝術叢書

・小畫家的天空系列・

活用不同的創作工具

靈活表現各種題材

讓青少年朋友動手又動腦

創造一個夢想的世界

國家圖書館出版品預行編目資料

前進白虎嶺 / Anna Fienberg,Barbara Fienberg著,Kim
　Gamble繪;王秋瑩譯.－－初版一刷.－－臺北市;
　三民,民90
　　面; 公分--(探索英文叢書.大喜說故事系列;6)
中英對照
ISBN 957-14-3416-7　(平裝)

1.英國語言—讀本

805.18　　　　　　　　　　　　90002913

網路書店位址　http://www.sanmin.com.tw

©　前進白虎嶺

著作人　Anna Fienberg　Barbara Fienberg
繪　圖　Kim Gamble
譯　者　王秋瑩
發行人　劉振強
著作財
產權人　三民書局股份有限公司
　　　　臺北市復興北路三八六號
發行所　三民書局股份有限公司
　　　　地址／臺北市復興北路三八六號
　　　　電話／二五〇〇六六〇〇
　　　　郵撥／〇〇〇九九九八——五號
印刷所　三民書局股份有限公司
門市部　復北店／臺北市復興北路三八六號
　　　　重南店／臺北市重慶南路一段六十一號
初版一刷　中華民國九十年四月
編　號　S 85584
定　價　新臺幣壹佰柒拾元
行政院新聞局登記證局版臺業字第〇二〇〇號

有著作權·不准侵害

ISBN　957-14-3416-7　(平裝)